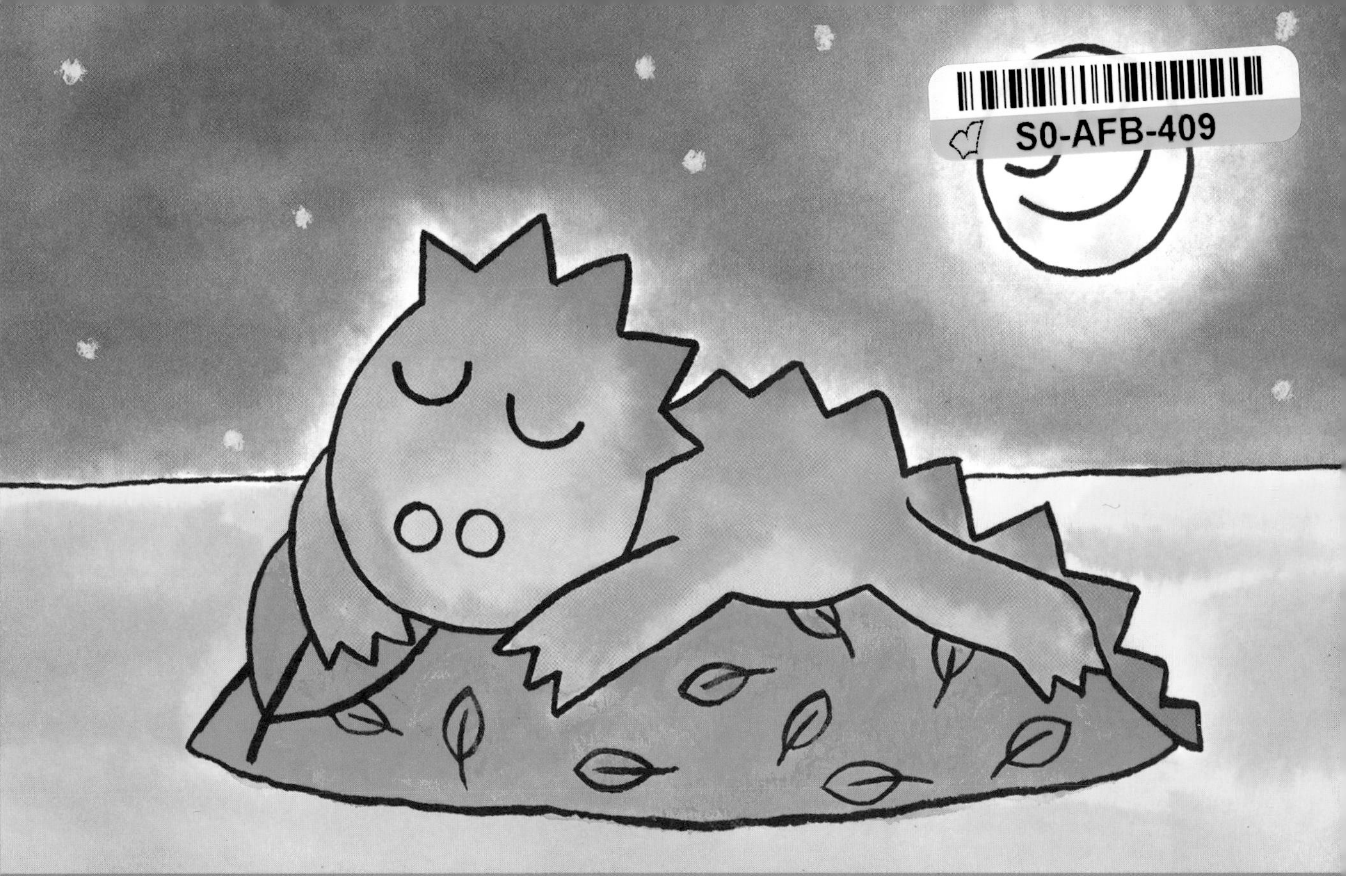

Dinah Dinosaur goes to sleep.

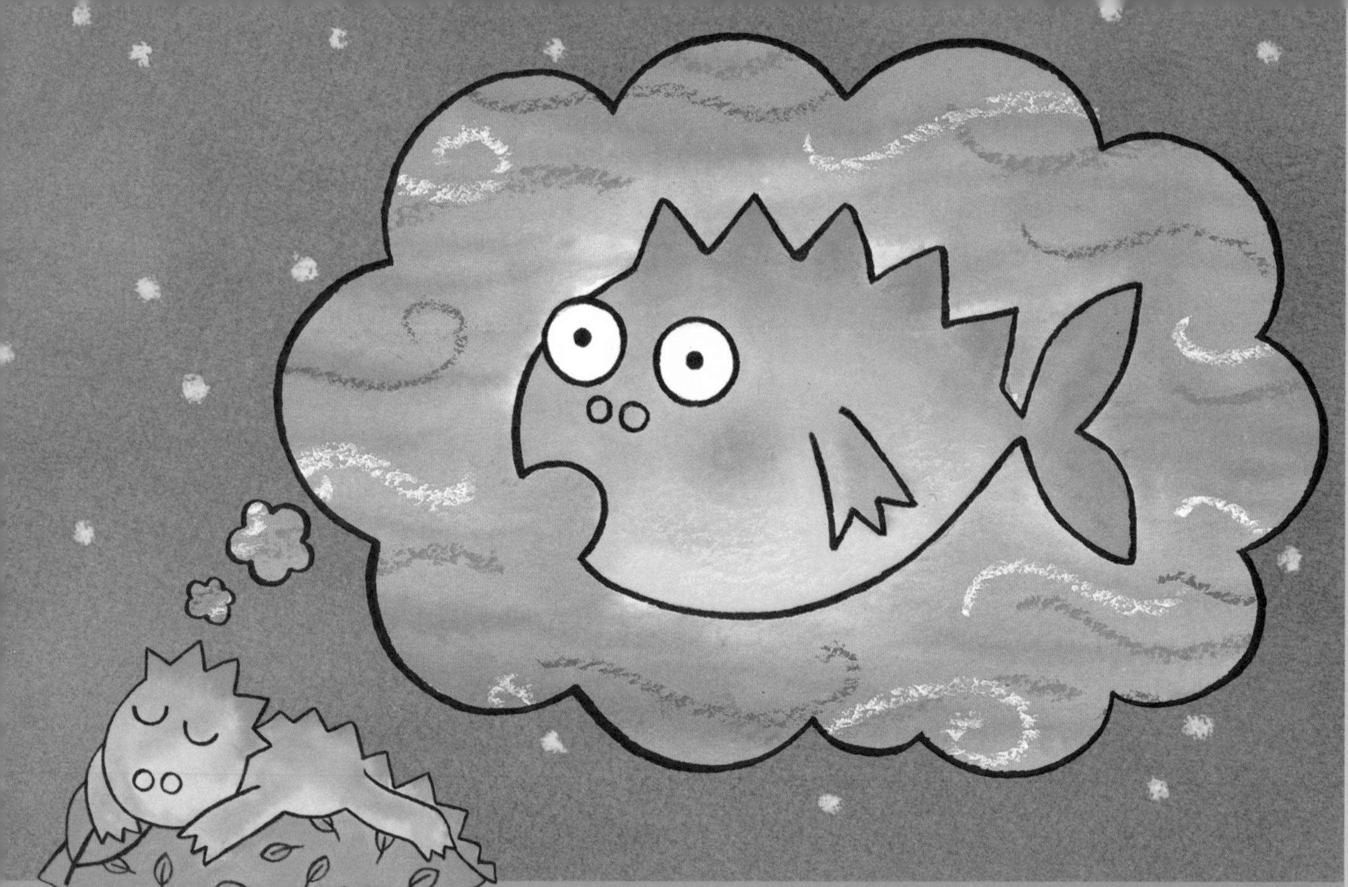

She dreams she is a fish.

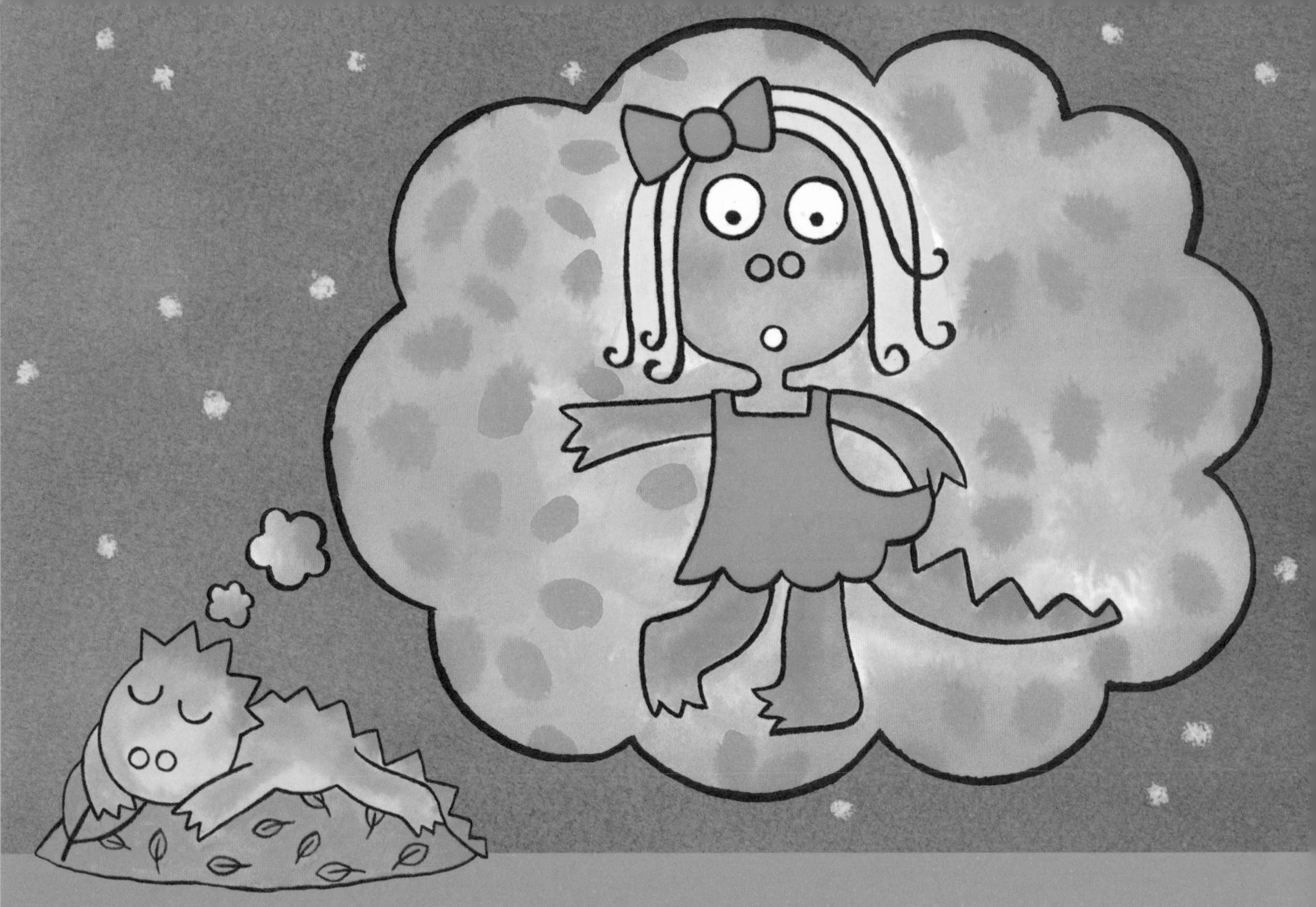

She dreams she is a girl.

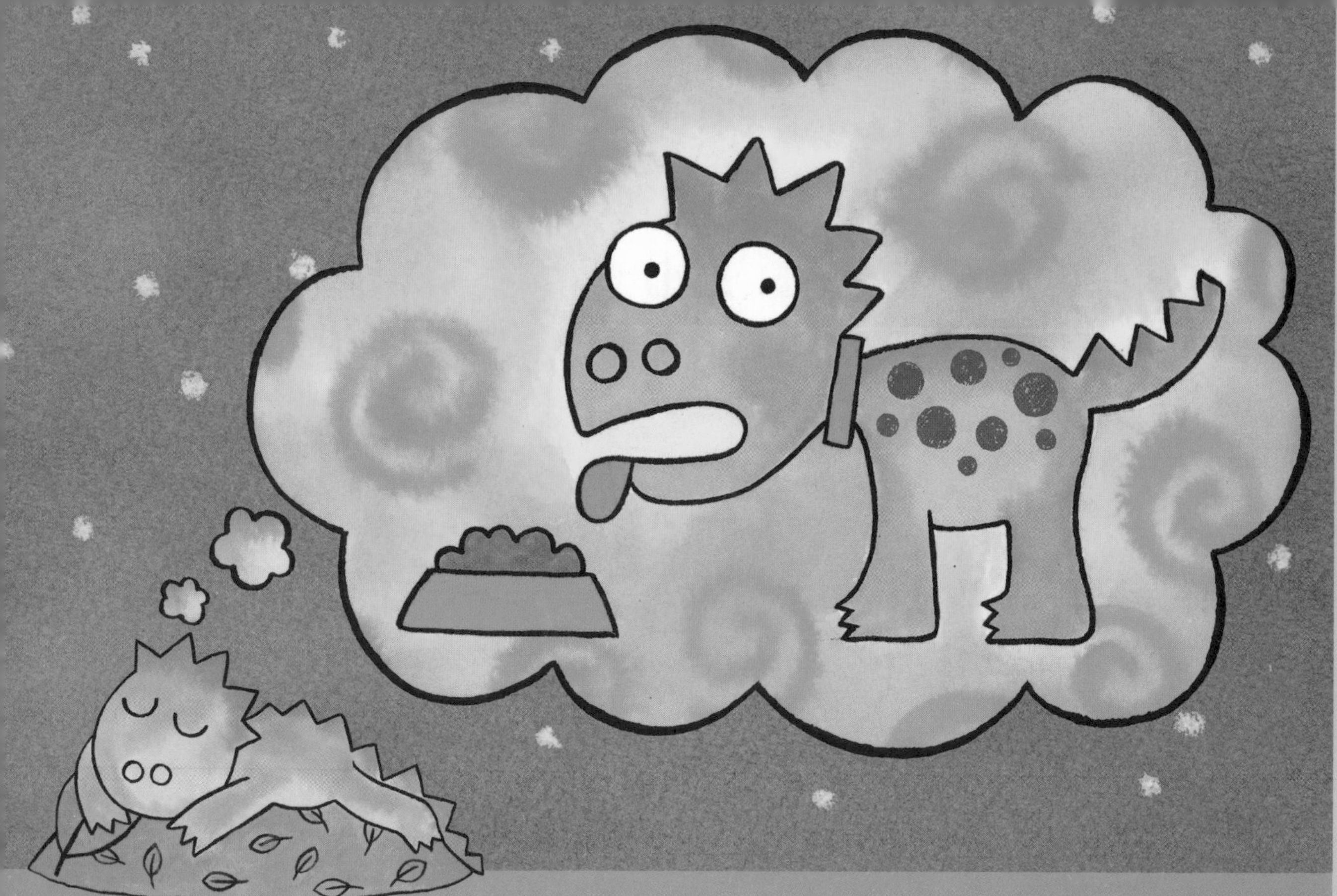

She dreams she is a dog.

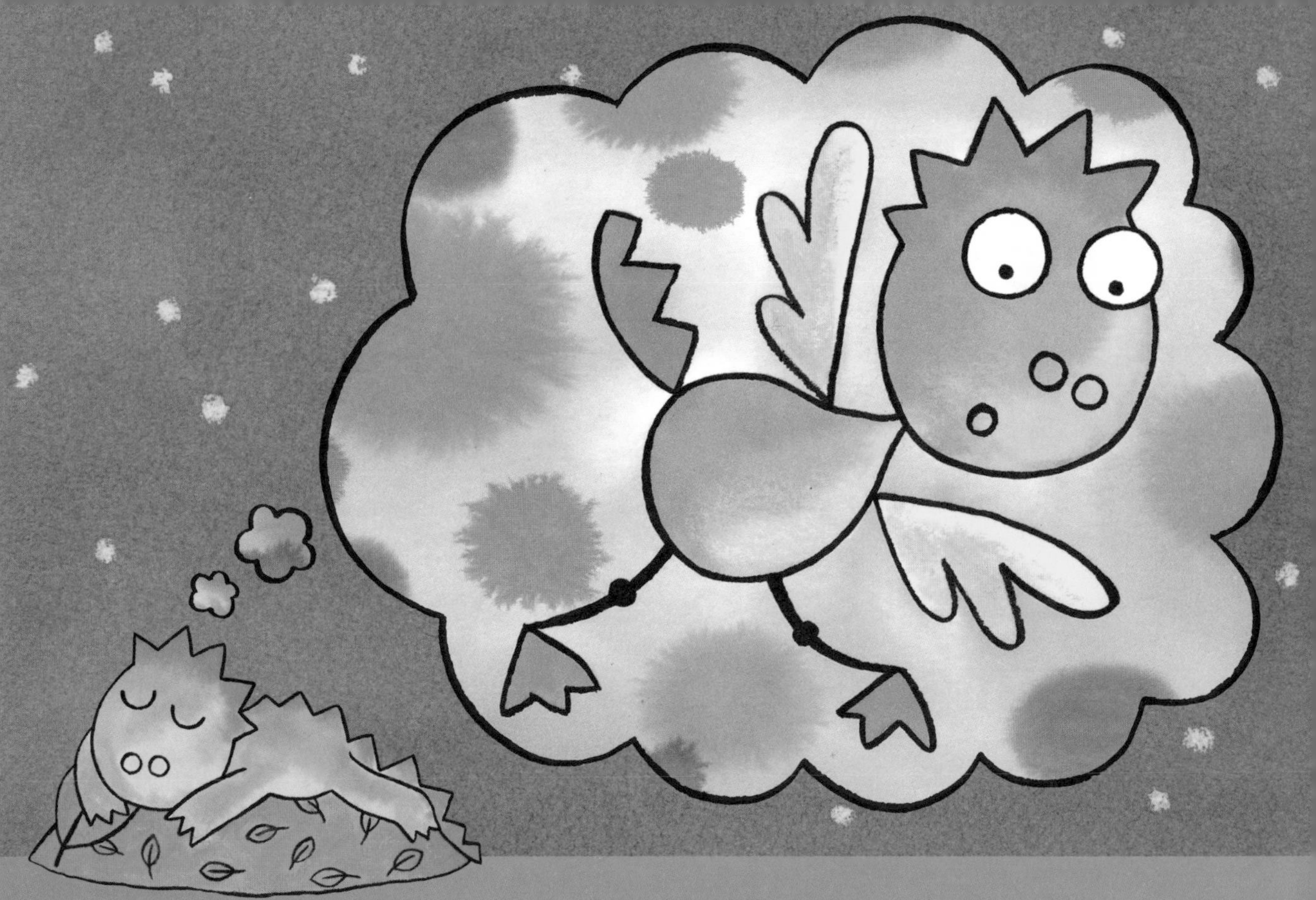

She dreams she is a bird.

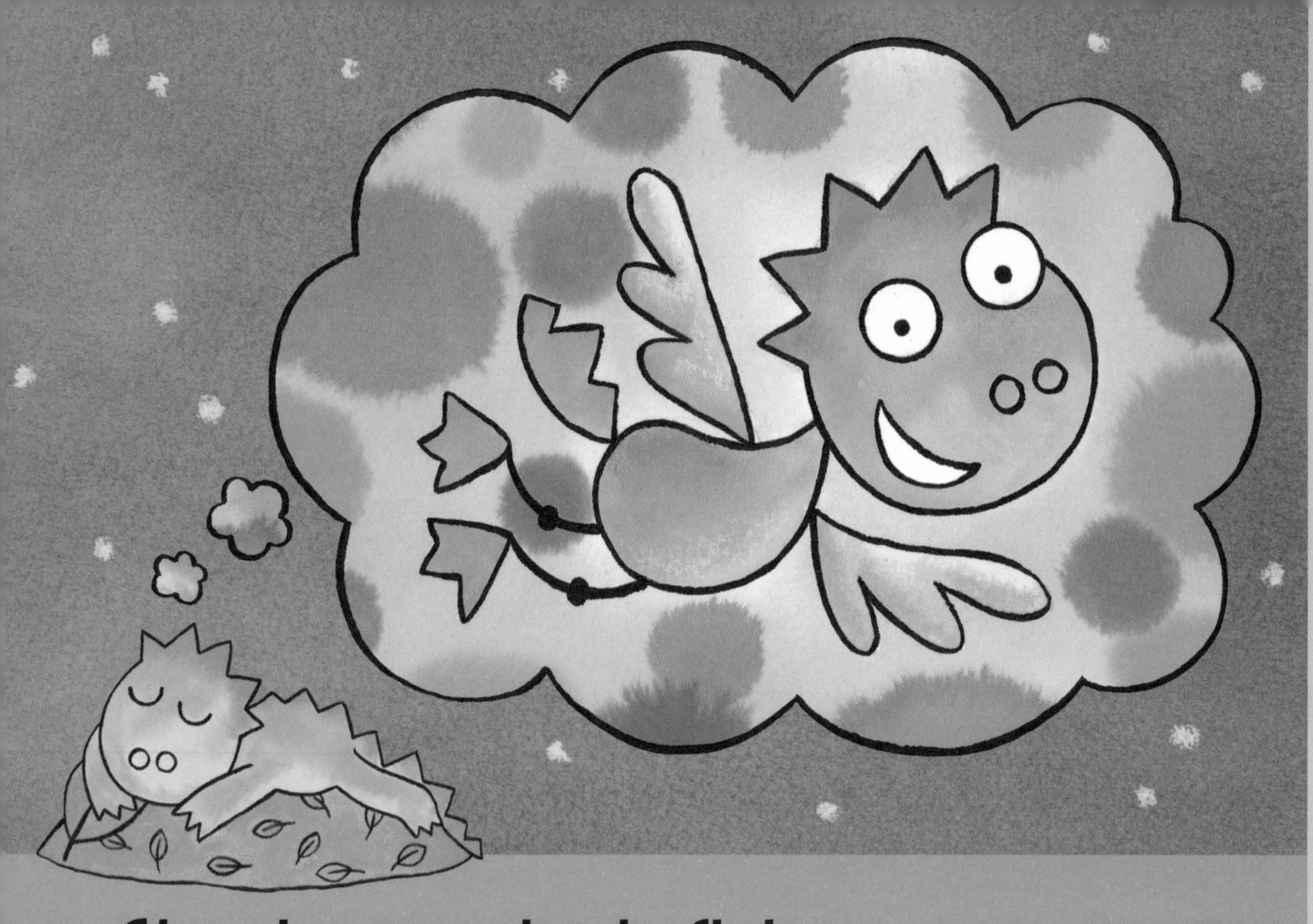

She dreams she is flying.

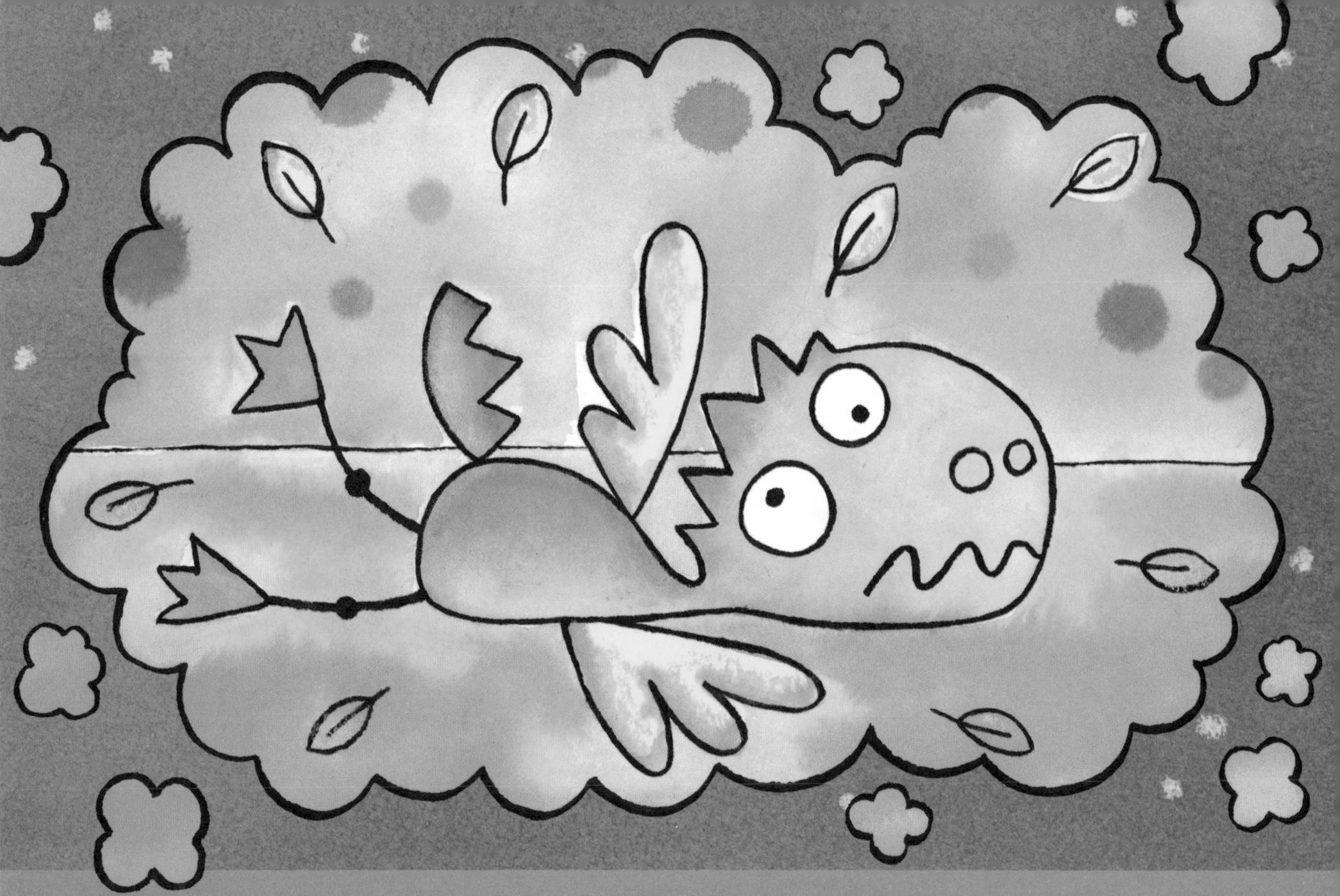

CRASH!

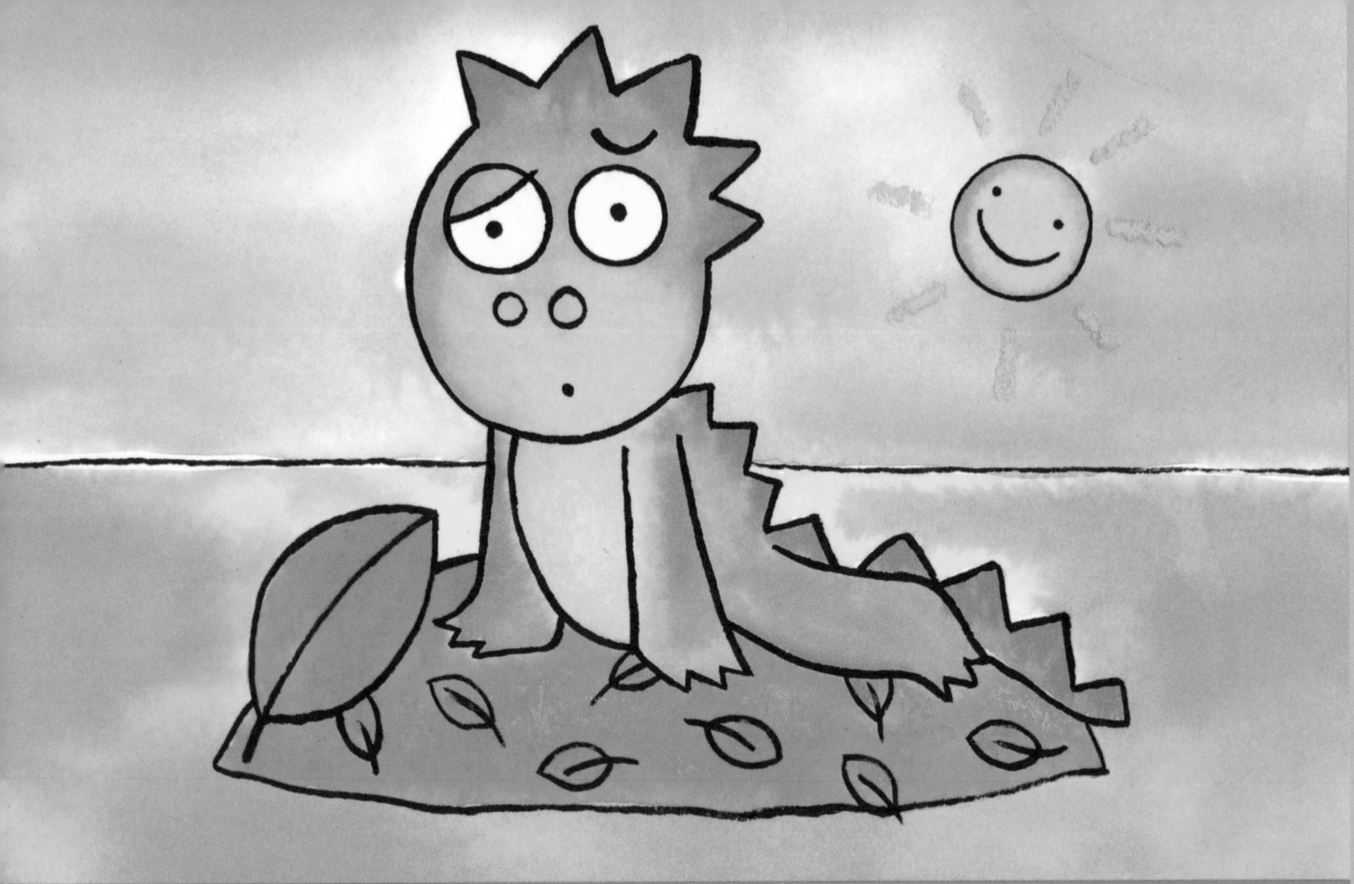

Dinah Dinosaur wakes up.